I dedicate this book to all the wonderful animals on this beautiful planet Earth

Heaven on Earth

Fleja the unicorn child, flying with her parents over the newborn, recovered planet Earth

Andrea Selina

Publishing house and distributed worldwide by:
tredition GmbH
Grindelallee 188, 20144 Hamburg, Germany
www.tredition.de

Paperback	ISBN 978-3-7323-3140-6
Hardcover	ISBN 978-3-7323-3141-3
E-Book	ISBN 978-3-7323-3142-0

www.tredition.de

Contents

Preface
Introduction

Preface

One of my visions is to help animals be more respected and loved as well as to help humanity recognize animals as their own souls on their own soul path. I also want to help them recover completely, including the whole of Mother Nature. We are all connected; we are all in the same "ship" sailing on planet Earth.

My visions became this story, in which a unicorn family flies with their daughter over the recently newborn planet Earth to meet some of the magnificent and awesome animals that live there, which shows us the unique gifts each of them presents to us.

I hope many people read this book and that it helps them recognize every single soul, including the souls of the animal kingdom and of Mother Earth as souls on their own soul paths. I wish that people will be able to respect them and find peace and unconditional love within themselves so that we, together, are able to create "Heaven on Earth".

Andrea

Introduction

Earth is going through a vast dimensional shift, moving from the third to the fifth dimension in a very short space of time.

We, as humans, share our planet with a vast and intricate array of beautiful beings... the animal kingdom.

Many souls have viewed the animals of this planet as a lesser species, as this attitude was established during the final years of Atlantis over 10,000 years ago. The reality of this couldn´t be more different.

Every animal soul on Earth is on its own and unique ascension path. And every single one of them has a vital role to play in the establishment and raising of the fifth dimensional vibration. It is also worth noting that at the time of my writing this introduction, over 75% of the animal kingdom has already achieved physical ascension.

Our relationship with the animals is changing as fast as the energy matrix. One of the highest heart facets that humans are tested on, is their love and empathy towards them.

Once we learn to love ourselves in our entirety, then we can truly love and respect the brave and selfless souls we have chosen to incarnate with.

I truly hope that you enjoy this beautiful story that my dear friend Andrea has written. Read the words carefully, and feel the vibration and message contained within.

Tim Whild

1. Africa: An Elephant Herd and a Pride of Lions

Fleja the unicorn child and her wise parents often flew over the beautiful, recently newborn planet Earth, spreading angelic light over the trees, plants, flowers, rivers and seas as well as over all the wonderful animals and warm hearted people that live there. After a long period of time, planet Earth had completely recovered. Wild animals were once again living free in their natural habitats, thankful that humanity had given them back their territories. Domestic animals were also living freely and harmoniously within their families, with everything necessary to be able to live, love and develop their own souls as well to have fun and serve their families, as is their free will, with all their decisions respected and communicated telepathically.

One sunny Morning, Fleja and her parents made a special visit to one of the vast herds of elephants in the middle of Africa with its profuse vegetation comprising lush bushes, majestic trees and all kinds of high and short grasses as well as waterholes, pools, lakes and streams. Nature was blooming in such magnificence that it made hearts jump for joy. As they softly landed beside the enormous herd, Jan, the wise old elephant soul and granny too many of the youngsters including the recently new-born calf Jumby, welcomed the unicorn family warmly. She hugged each one softly with her trunk as the unicorns gave her a loving touch with their brightly shimmering horns.

"Hello Nuja, hello Flynn and hello beautiful Fleja! What a pleasure to see you today! And thank you for hearing my telepathic invitation! We are so pleased with our Jumby and I am soooo excited to introduce you to him today," said Jan joyfully.

"Hello lovely Jan, nice to see you, too," the unicorns replied together.

"Is it true that I can play with Jumby today?" Fleja asked shyly.

"Yes Fleja. He will be very happy to play with you," Jan answered lovingly. "Now, let's go and see my large family. They'll all certainly be very happy to see you!"

They moved cheerfully toward the mighty herd, passing the many elephant families who greeted the unicorns with much joy and love in their eyes. "Jan, how have you been doing since our last visit? Is everything okay with you and your big family? Are all the elephants well?" Nuja asked.

"Thank you Nuja. Yes, all is well and everybody is very happy. The vast landscape nourishes us in every way and we have enough healthy water to drink and for our daily cleansing bath. Nature supports us with so much love and generosity. We are so grateful."

In the middle of the herd, safely protected by the other family members, was Jumby, the newborn calf and his overjoyed mother, Amy. "Hello Nuja, hello Flynn, hello Fleja. Welcome and thank you for visiting us! May I introduce you to my lovely baby, Jumby." Jumby smiled shyly toward the unicorns, still cuddling his mother's legs by gently rubbing one ear after the other along her stomach.

"Hello Amy and hello Jumby!" Nuja said. Nuja carefully touched Jumby's forehead with her rainbow colored horn as Jumby leapt and smiled brightly.

"Dear Jumby, may I introduce you to Fleja. She will be very happy to play with you today," Amy added.

"Hello Jumby," Fleja said shyly.

"Hello Fleja," Jumby answered, carefully walking outside his mother's big legs toward his new friend. They smiled brightly into each other's eyes and after a short, loving touch of the horn to the trunk and the trunk to the horn, promptly started to run and play together joyfully.

The elephant herd continued to walk across a landscape full of grass, trees and all kinds of food such as roots, leaves and branches. Nuja, Flynn, Jan, Amy and Jumbo, Jumby's father, walked slowly onward, exchanging the latest experiences and discussing good news, while Jumby and Fleja got to know each other. "Fleja, why is your horn shimmering so softly in such beautiful colors and why does it feel so tingly when you touch me with it?" Jumby asked.

"It is because our horns are pure radiant light. They pour out pure love and healing energy to everything they come into contact with," Fleja answered wisely.

"Oh, that sounds really great," Jumby said.

"Jumby, could you please tell me what you can do with your big trunk … it looks so sweet!" Fleja asked.

"Oh, my trunk is really great," Jumby answered, smiling mischievously from ear to ear as he quickly scooped up a little sandy earth and sprayed it in great style over his body, before trumpeting as loudly as possible and smiling brightly toward Fleja. Fleja started to laugh so hard that tears ran down her cheeks. Jumby repeated his show.

"That is so funny," chuckled Fleja.

Fleja and Jumby followed their families, playing hide and seek between the elephant herd, spreading joy, laughter and happiness. As they reached a big pool, filled within clear, pure, sparkling water for drinking and bathing, Fleja, Jumby and the other children started running into it, bathing, paddling, cuddling and playing together joyfully. Jumby and his playfellows sucked up water with their trunks, then entwined them together and squirted the water over themselves. Others rolled from one side to the other, trumpeting and laughing as many elephants cuddled together with indescribable love and joy.

Fleja left the pool and joined her parents on the bank. They all watched this happy spectacle, laughing until their bodies ached and their horns radiated pure white light of unconditional love. Gradually, several of the adult elephants joined in the spectacle, bathing and splashing like the youngsters, while others stayed and watched, protecting the herd and keeping a watchful eye on the children. The elephants loved playing with the children. But they also protected them carefully, caring for their health, development, joy and happiness. None of the children was ever left alone or unprotected.

Once every elephant was clean and satisfied, the herd rested near the pool on the soft sandy earth. Some simply talked or slept, guarded by the wise old elephants. After Jumby had received his milk from his adoring mommy, he also decided to sleep. Later, as he and Fleja started to play together again by running between the herd, they discovered a male lion lying on a big limb of a tree, watching over his pride. Hungry for knowledge, they immediately ran back to their parents.

"Mommy, Daddy," Jumby called breathlessly as they reached them. "May Fleja and I visit the pride of lions in the neighborhood near the trees?"

Amy and Jumbo smiled proudly at the curiosity and thirst for knowledge on Jumby's face. Fleja also asked her parents, and after a short discussion, both sets of parents decided to allow them to visit, but only if the dads accompanied them. Cheerfully, all four walked toward the end of the herd, singing the elephant's hymn quietly.

"Hello Ted." Jumbo and Flynn greeted the male lion, who, with a friendly smile, raised his head to show his magnificent mane.

"Hello Jumbo, hello Flynn. And hello children. What a pleasure to see you all here. How are you?"

"Well, thank you Ted. We're just fantastic! How are you?" Jumbo asked.

"All is well," Ted replied.

"May I introduce you to my son Jumby and his playmates Fleja, Flynn and Nuja's girl. The children wanted to visit you ... would that be okay for you and your pride?"

"Oh yes, Jumbo, that would be nice."

"Thank you Ted," Jumbo and Flynn answered gratefully.

"Well, Jumby, Fleja, what can I do for you? Do you want to visit our kindergarten?" Ted asked gently.

"Yes!" Jumby and Fleja answered simultaneously.

Ted jumped masterfully from the tree and roared mightily toward the lion's pride as Jumbo and Flynn waited in a safe place nearby. Confidently and with a majestic stride, Ted then walked together with Fleja and Jumby to the legendary lion kindergarten, which was circled by a few of the lionesses, who took care of the lion cubs and suckled them if they were hungry. All lion mothers together are responsible for all the children in a pride and each one gives their milk regardless. It makes no difference to the lionesses. They love all the cubs without condition and they love being mothers.

It was a beautiful day. The sun was glistening through the trees, which framed the wonderful meadow in which all the lion cubs were playing, jumping and making up all kinds of games. They nuzzled the ears of their playfellows softly, playfully jumping on the backs of the lionesses and sliding down, rough-and-tumbled or simply rolled on their backs while chortling gleefully. The atmosphere was warm, peaceful, harmonic and safe. While some of the other adult lions watched over the herd and guarded the landscape, the rest were simply having a catnap. Everything worked well, calmly, peacefully and telepathically.

As Ted, Fleja and Jumby reached the lion kindergarten, the cubs and mothers smiled and welcomed them. Fleja and Jumby greeted them happily. Ted then softly spoke to the lion cubs. "My lovelies, may I introduce you to the unicorn child, Fleja, and her playfellow Jumby. They would be delighted to play with you today. As you know, unicorns and elephants do not have fur, just a thin skin, and so please be careful! Don't bite them or use your claws while you are playing. Will this work for you, guys?"

"Yes, yes, yes, we will be careful," all the lion cubs answered swiftly.

They instantly moved toward Fleja and Jumby, sniffing and touching them and beginning to play together, running in a circle, jumping, cuddling and rolling in the meadow. Shortly afterwards, the rest of the adult lions came back with a group of lion teens who had been on a trip together learning about their environment, improving their skills and talents and using their strength wisely. All were excited about their trip and very pleased to met Fleja and Jumby in the lion kindergarten.

Later in the afternoon, Jumbo and Flynn slowly moved toward the pride. They gently called: "Fleja, Jumby, we have to go home to our families now. Please say goodbye to the lions and thank them."

Jumbo and Fleja thanked the lions for being such great hosts: "Thank you, thank you dear lions! We have to go now. Bye, thank you bye, bye."

"Bye, thank you for your visit," came the lions' joyful response in chorus.

Jumbo and Flynn also thanked the lions for taking care of the children, and soon the four of them, with sparkling eyes, were walking back to the elephant herd, which had camped beside the big pool for the night. Nuja, Jan and Amy welcomed them on their return.

"How was your afternoon with the lions?" Amy asked.

Fleja and Jumby, still with sparkling eyes, smiled brightly toward them and said in chorus: "Woooooonderful!"

Everyone started to laugh. Jumby and Fleja then lay down side by side and fell asleep.

The next morning, they awoke to a beautiful sunrise. After a morning bath in the pool with Amy, Jan, Jumbo and Jumby, Flynn, Nuja and Fleja said goodbye to the elephant herd, spreading their angelic light over them, as the elephants trumpeted a wonderful hymn together. The unicorns once again surrounded them, radiating pure sparkles of golden light. Blissfully, the elephant herd continued their journey across the beautiful landscape, while the unicorn family flew toward Europe, enjoying the refreshing wind.

2. Alps: A Herd of Cows

As they flew over Europe, the environment seemed to be totally rejuvenated, newly arisen like a Phoenix from the Ashes. Beautiful green landscapes with wild flowers and hedges and deciduous, coniferous and mixed forests covered vast tracts of the land. Clear water, lakes, rivers and streams glistened in the sunlight, reflecting the green nature surrounding them. Repetitive cultivation over vast areas had now vanished and it was replaced with beautiful vegetables, fruit trees and cereal fields. Because humanity had now recognized that every animal has a soul (and a soul journey) just like humans, there is no more need to cultivate fattening feed. At last, the vast landscapes had been returned to Mother Nature.

Bumblebees and many other magnificent insects buzzed around the beautiful green pastures while singing and working hard, blissfully happy to serve nature and all its inhabitants on this wonderful planet Earth. What's more, all the chemical fertilizers, pesticides and plant protection products had vanished. Humans now understood that there was absolutely no need for any such products, which harmed nature, humans and the whole animal kingdom. With love, compassion and the necessary knowledge, the plants were now growing much better than ever and nourished at a superior level.

After a short flight, Flynn, Nuja and Fleja reached the Alps, landing gently in a wonderful mountain pasture where healthy herds of cows with their calves grazed between small herds of goats and sheep, all enjoying the rich green pastures, the fresh air and the warming sunrays on this wonderful spring day.

"Hello everybody." Flynn, Nuja and Fleja greeted the familiar herds around them with a gentle smile and activated their horns, showering radiant light across the herds and pasture with celestial bliss.

"Hello, hello" was heard from every side, from all the amazing and different voices.

Flynn and Nuja walked toward their friends Betty and Laura, while Fleja ran joyfully to the calf playgroup, founded by the calves themselves shortly after they were born, which was always carefully protected within the whole herd. "Hello guys. May I join your game? Fleja asked breathlessly."

"Of course, Fleja," the calves answered happily, and one after the other they welcomed her and touched her softly, before continuing their play.

Flynn, Nuja, Betty and Laura, who were both mothers of the calves, watched this loving spectacle, feeling overjoyed and proud.

"This really is a joy to watch," Nuja said.

Laura replied: "Yes, Nuja, we love these playgroups, too. They give us so much love and joy. I can't even comprehend it. It all started automatically since we are free, living in nature again and able to suckle our calves with our milk. This milk is so special and important for them because it includes all the necessary vitamins and antibodies."

Betty added: "This special milk enables the calves to reconnect with our ancient knowledge and wisdom much easier and it helps them grow at every level of life. It is our inherent gift from Source. Our kids show love and empathy to each other in the playgroups. It is such a big love to discern."

"I am really pleased to hear and see these wonderful changes," Nuja said, enthusiastically.

"Yes, the changes are so magnificent! We are feeling so wonderful and just awesome. Indeed, humans also benefit from our new lifestyle as our milk, which we freely share with them, is now much more compatible for them as we are herbivores. Finally, we have the ability to eat only organic food without concentrated foodstuffs, just as it was always planned. As humans started to respect us as the animals we really are, with a soul and a soul path of our own, and with the ability to love and serve, they also changed their demands. They stopped trying to get as much milk as possible from us and stopped cutting our horns, which are part of our nervous system and very important for our wellbeing and for the shared milk as well. We are now able to live our life with joy, happiness and much more love."

They all spent a wonderful relaxed day together, enjoying the sun and the singing of crickets and birds as well as the steady calmness of the majestic mountains encircling the beautiful pastures. From time to time, some of the younger calves came to their mothers to drink or have a cuddle, while other cows and calves spent time sleeping or walking around the landscape. Later, in the early evening, as some of the cows shared milk with the humans at the local pastures, they also enjoyed the love and gratitude shown by the dairy farmers. Soon afterwards, after eating and drinking as much grass and water as they wished, the cows, sheep, goats and unicorn family watched a gorgeous sunset.

"What a beautiful relaxed day! Thank you so much for this, dear friends," Nuja said to the cows, sheep and goats. Then, they all lay down together for a wonderful, healthy sleep under the rising stars.

3. Hungary and Romania: A Herd of Wild Horses

The next morning, just before sunrise, Flynn, Nuja and Fleja said goodbye to the lovely herds of cows, sheep and goats and continued their journey toward Hungary and Romania to a vast herd of wild horses that had again become popular from Europe through to Mongolia as well as on the other continents. Because the horses were their soul sisters, living in an embodied form on Mother Earth, the unicorn family was very excited to meet them.

The grass was still wearing its fresh cloak from the morning dew, as they softly touched down. "Hello Nuja, hello Flynn, hello Fleja. What a delight to welcome you," Ron, one of the stallions, greeted them lovingly.

"Hello Ron, nice to see you again. I hope you have had a lot of fun since our last meeting," Flynn answered.

"Yes Flynn, I have. Our lives are stunning now we are able to live them as it was always planned. Look into our eyes and you can see the beauty and love we share with everyone and everything we meet."

Nuja and Fleja joined the herd, greeting and touching them lovingly by using their ears or horns. They started to communicate telepathically while Ron and Flynn continued to talk. Fleja quickly merged with a group of foals playing together, and they all started a race from one end of the herd to the other, running, jumping, laughing and having so much fun.

Later that morning, the whole herd commenced their daily run over the vast landscape, speeding over the green meadows along the forests and rivers, jumping over obstacles and small streams, enjoying the wind in their manes, feeling pure liberty. They were letting go of the old and enjoying their timelessness, living in the moment, just being and feeling their oneness with nature, with the earth and the air. It was pure fun and joy.

"What fun this is, I have really missed it," Flynn said to Ron cheerfully while heading toward a beautiful meadow to rest and meet some of their domestic fellows living with humans nearby.

"Hi, nice to see you," Flynn greeted the domestic horses.

"Hi Flynn! What a pleasure to see you, too. How are you?" Tony, one of the domestic stallions, asked.

"Fine Tony. We have had a lot of fun with our daughter Fleja and are enjoying a journey across Earth visiting animal families. How are you and your fellows doing?"

"All is perfect, Flynn, now we are able to go for a free run as often as we like and we have beautiful clean stables. We love to return to our domestic homes as well as to our human families. You know, we love them all, especially the children who are so sensitive and loving like ourselves. Some of us serve them as healers, while others simply give them rides on our backs without a saddle and reins. The people have learned to trust us completely, as we trust them. Most of them hold onto our manes to keep balance, while others simply hold our necks gently and enjoy the ride."

"That's really fantastic, Tony. It is so wonderful to hear. We horses are all healers of a kind, especially for children. We have the ability to touch the souls of everybody and to send out healing through our mighty presence. It is our inherent gift! We have great sensitivity and unconditional love for everything and everyone alive."

"Yes, you said it Flynn! I can't express what a pleasure it is to watch our foals playing with the children. They are best friends and you see no difference between human and animal playmates ... it is very funny to watch," Tony laughed.

"Haha, that is really funny. I think every one of us can learn from them," Flynn replied.

After resting and talking with their fellows, the herd of wild horses and the unicorn family said goodbye to the domestic horses and proceeded on their run toward a beautiful fertile clearing on the forest's edge. They spent the rest of the day by a small stream, while taking the chance to run free and enjoy a fresh feast of grass and herbs.

"Running with the herd is so funny, Mommy," Fleja gasped breathlessly after they reached the clearing.

"Yes, Fleja, I like it too. I enjoy it time and time again when we meet one of these herds of wild horses, living freely, on this wonderful planet Earth," Nuja answered gently, thankful that her daughter was so happy.

Soon after dawn, Fleja and the foals lay down, overtired and promptly fell into a deep sleep that lasted the whole night.

The next morning, just before sunrise, they all enjoyed an early run together. Flynn looked toward Fleja and called: "It is time to say goodbye, Fleja."

Fleja immediately turned to her new friends. "Bye bye my friends, and thank you for this awesome playtime! See you soon."

The foals nodded their heads and waved their ears as the unicorn family flew away to the East.

4. India and Pakistan: A Family of Tigers

The weather was mild and sunny, and the unicorns enjoyed their journey over the beautiful green pastures, over the clear Bosporus filled with fish and over the beautiful and fertile landscapes of Iraq, Iran and Afghanistan, where the people lived peacefully together in their newly created environment. Humans were thankful for the reforestation of the forests, for the many water streams, for the abundant vegetable gardens and, of course, for the famous Persian gardens inviting people from all over the world to visit and meditate.

Shortly after noon, the unicorn family arrived at their planned destination: a wonderful fertile clearing with all kinds of jungle grasses, flowers and native herbs in one of the jungles that expanded from Pakistan, India and Nepal to Thailand. They had planned to meet a popular tiger family that was very excited about their visit and was already waiting for them in the clearing. As the largest species of the cat family, tigers are strong protectors, not only of their kids, but also of their whole district and Mother

Earth, too. They really appreciate the universe.

"Hey everybody!" Flynn greeted the Tiger family. Their cute playful cubs tumbled and rolled over themselves.

"Hey loved ones! You are very welcome!" Toro, the father of the cubs, answered lovingly. They all greeted each other warmly by touching their heads with the unicorns' horns. This seemed very funny to the tiger cubs.

"Let us walk to our cave nearby, loved ones. It is big enough for all of us and we can spend a wonderful time together there," Mini, the tigress, said.

They all walked together, interrupted only by the cute games of the cubs, eventually finding a cave hidden behind some large trees and bushes. In the cave, Mini, Nuja, Fleja and the four cubs proceeded to play, cuddling and hugging each other happily, while Flynn and Toro had a wise talk. The whole cave was filled with love and happiness.

As night set in, the unicorn family, the cubs and Mini went to sleep. Toro left the cave, as protector, to make sure all was well in the district, elegantly setting one paw atop the other. The next morning, they bathed in a clear fresh stream and Flynn, Nuja and Fleja thanked the tiger family for its hospitality before proceeding with their journey toward the Himalayas.

5. Himalayas: A Gaggle of Geese

High in the blue and fresh sky, the unicorns met a wonderful gaggle of geese flying shortly before dawn. Their trip went from southern India toward Central Asia over the vast Himalayas to their breeding sites.

"Hey there! Nice to meet you!" The geese greeted the unicorns in chorus, overjoyed by this unplanned meeting.

"Hey, loved ones." The unicorns quickly changed their planned route to fly with these wonderful birds who sprinkle unconditional love showers and radiate warmth over the lands as they fly, enjoying the wind and clear air. Geese are careful and compassionate. They love their family members unconditionally and look after each other. Furthermore, they have a very strong community spirit, which is crucial for such long and exhausting flights over this amazing mountain range.

To be certain that they did not disturb the perfect V formation of the geese, the unicorns flew a few feet above them, all the while chatting with each other about the latest news. They flew over this breathtaking Holy land, over the giant mountains and over the Indian Herakhan Kailash and Tibetian Kailash, where the beloved Holy Ones have their etheric retreats and local meditation places, emanating love, light and bliss over the whole Earth and its dwellers. Since Tibet was free again, shining in its glorious and divine presence as it was always meant to be, the whole planet was free, resurrected, rejuvenated. It was in full bloom, radiating love, compassion, abundance, safety and warmth for all its inhabitants.

6. China: Pandas and Domestic Pigs

Still enjoying this Divinity, the geese and unicorn family said goodbye. Flynn, Nuja and Fleja changed their course again and flew toward China to visit the vast bamboo forests on the border with Tibet and to catch a view of the beautiful pandas that live there permanently. The reforested bamboo and beautiful crystal clear and fresh mountain views made a beautiful landscape and a unique paradise as well.

"Hello, lovely ones," Fleja greeted a group of beautiful pandas, eating bamboo, as they flew over them.

"Hello, lovely unicorns! Nice to see you," the pandas greeted back, happy and excited to see them.

"Let us fly over the whole area, Flynn, and bless these nice and beautiful bears as well as this wonderful nature with our horns," Nuja said. The unicorns started to fly in circles, becoming larger and larger until they covered the giant bamboo forests and its neighborhood with their blissful presence and blessings.

"That's marvelous and makes me so happy!" Fleja said, overjoyed, concentrating on touching every single panda child with her radiating light.

"You did a great job Fleja!" Flynn said smiling with pride and delight about their wonderful healing.

"Okay Fleja, we are ready now. Let us say goodbye to the nice pandas and proceed on our journey," Nuja said, still radiating love and light with her horn.

"Bye beautiful pandas," Fleja called over the whole area. The pandas thanked them and waved goodbye.

The unicorn family proceeded with their journey toward south China, happy to recognize that the pigpens and cultivated fields for animal feed had vanished, replaced with fresh forests, nature parks, fruit and vegetable plantations and many small streams, all supporting wild and domestic animals as well as the people in the surrounding countries. Humanity had finally recognized that animals are on their own soul journeys here on Earth and have not chosen to incarnate as food for humans. Pigs on Earth were now respected for their love, compassion and healing energy, which they brought as a gift from the be-loved Pleiades. Some of them now live free in their areas, whereas others have chosen to live as domestic animals within families, enjoying life on Earth with all its beauty.

After such a busy day, Flynn, Nuja and Fleja looked for a calm, comfortable sleep-ing place on one of the paradisiacal white sandy beaches in Vietnam. With beauty and grace, they lay down between the palms on the soft green grass.

"Oh, how wonderful! We will sleep and dream here very well, enjoying the healthy salty sea air," Nuja said happily, and soon they all fell into a deep sleep.

7. Bali: The Isle of the Gods

Early the next morning, Flynn, Nuja and Fleja flew toward Australia over fresh clear oceans and beautiful islands. Soon, they passed the magical, calm and majestic island of Bali. "The Isle of the Gods" was famous for its beautiful rice terraces, blooming gardens, monkey forests, holy temple complexes and endless sandy beaches, radiating a unique divine atmosphere and vibe far beyond its borders.

"Oh, that is beautiful," Fleja said, astonished.

"Yes Fleja, this is such a beautiful place, made with love and a sense of grace and respect for the plants and environment, simultaneously honoring the Divinity in every single thing. It really is Heaven on Earth," Nuja said proudly.

8. Australia: Uluru, Kangaroos and Koalas

Back above the vast Pacific Ocean, Nuja, Flynn and Fleja watched a school of beautiful, majestic sharks swimming on the surface of the sea, just having fun together while circling and diving before resurfacing above the waves.

"Hi lovely sharks. How are you?" Fleja asked.

"Very well, unicorn child, thank you dear. We are having fun together with our kids and brothers and sisters of the sea," answered Timmy, one of the elders, joyfully.

"How nice to hear that Timmy and how nice to meet you all. Have a nice day, bye, bye!"

"Thanks, I wish you all a good and lovely trip. Hope to see you again soon," Timmy replied.

After receiving more blessings from the horns of the unicorns, Fleja, Nuja and Flynn continued on their journey. As the unicorns reached the beautiful continent of Australia, they again poured their Divine light showers over the landscape below, acknowledging the amazing changes now that all of humanity is respecting Mother Earth and all her animals.

Non-invasive agricultural devices are now used to preserve the soil and allow it, in its natural organic rhythm, to rejuvenate. As a result, the whole continent is able to grow and blossom again, including the driest regions, rising up like a Phoenix from the Ashes. Above majestic Uluru, this vast monolith with its unique colors and appearance affected by the sunlight, they gave a special thanks to the Divine. Uluru is an important spiritual place for the Dreamtime of the Aborigines, embedded in its local flora and fauna. It has finally closed for hiking tours and it is now allowed to rest in its Divine presence, as it was always meant to be.

A kangaroo group with breeding females carrying their young in their special pouches on their bodies, lovely youngsters and several adult males were joyfully hopping around nearby, having fun and enjoying the moment. "Hi beautiful kangaroos!" Flynn, Nuja and Fleja greeted them with friendly smiles.

"Hi beautiful unicorns," the kangaroos, overwhelmed with joy, called back to them.

The sun still stood in the midst of Heaven as they softly landed in one of the many reforested eucalyptus woods in the east of Australia. They met beautiful and sensitive koalas living in the trees, which provided their homes, their sleeping places and their food. The bushfires had now decreased by reducing agricultural areas and new, earth friendly systems were sparing the soil and helping regenerate and nourish nature. Vast reforesting programs had restored many plants, flowers and insects such as bees and ants as well as larger animals. The drier climate has totally vanished and great, newly connected landscapes had emerged, allowing the population of these beautiful koalas to recover gradually.

Fleja and her parents first decided to rest under some of these beautiful eucalyptus trees, enjoying the warmth and stillness of this wonderful space before chatting with the koala families. Shortly before sunset, Tessy, the koala mom with her baby Tini in her pouch, slowly walked from the neighborhood, after having enjoyed a cleansing and warm cuddle together, toward her sister Meg's eucalyptus tree area to meet the unicorn family.

"Hello, you're so welcome!" Meg and Tessy tenderly greeted the unicorns now they were all awake and rested.

"Hello Meg, hello Tessy. Nice to see you again and how gracious of you to meet us on the ground as well," Nuja said softly.

"It is an honor to meet you here, dear Nuja, although we are not very good walkers on the ground. As we get most of our water from the eucalyptus leaves, there is no need to be on the ground often," Tessy said.

"How was your journey until now?" Meg added.

"Oh we have really enjoyed it. The new Earth looks so beautiful. The whole of nature is regenerating and blooming in all its glory," Nuja answered.

"So nice to hear from you, dear Nuja. We are also enjoying our new climate and we are much healthier than before," Meg said shyly. Tini's fluffy ears appeared from out of her mom's pouch and the baby offered a warm welcoming smile.

"Hello Tini," Fleja tenderly welcomed the baby with a bright smile and a lovely touch and shower with her horn, filled with infinite love and blessings. Tini was overjoyed and smiled brightly back at Fleja, tenderly cuddling her mom's tummy.

The stars rose and they all enjoyed a radiant starlit night with a beautiful moon in the sky. Fleja soon fell asleep, and after they said goodbye to each other, the koalas returned to their eucalyptus trees to slowly and appreciatively chew eucalyptus leaves while the unicorns had a relaxing sleep.

9. Oceans: Dolphins and Whales

Soon after dawn, Fleja and her parents continued toward the coast of New Zealand, flying above a magnificent school of dolphins just breaching the water's surface. "Hey lovely dolphins," Fleja greeted them happily, enjoying the fresh sea breeze above the water.

"Hey Fleja, nice to see you, too," Dicki, a big blue-gray dolphin, called back while swimming and stretching his beautiful smiling face toward Fleja.

"We are going to cross the Pacific Ocean toward South America, Dicki. It would be a pleasure if you and your dolphin friends were able to join us for a while. I do love your spreading joy and love so much!"

"Thanks for the compliments. I would really appreciate that. It would be an honor to join you marvelous unicorns. Let me just ask my friends."

Dicki communicated telepathically with his dolphin friends and immediately they all agreed. Happily and with much fun, Fleja and her parents proceeded on their journey, while the dolphins swam in the sea below, playfully and joyfully jumping, looping in the air, just enjoying the moment and following the flow. The unicorns flew low in the air above them, grateful for such loving companions and happy at the indescribable joy and unconditional love the dolphins were sending out to the universe and all its dwellers.

"Hey Fleja, would you like a little cold water?" Dicki laughed. As soon as his words had been spoken, he made a huge splash into the water so that Fleja was touched by a soft ocean shower.

"Hey Dicki, I like that!" she called.

"I know Fleja! That's why I did it!"

The clear water was glistening in the sun, reflecting the purity. All the pollution in the sea and oceans had vanished as soon as everybody on Earth took responsibility for his or her own actions and helped clean up the pollution. As they reached the beautiful and clean South Sea Islands, the dolphins turned back.

"Bye, bye, Fleja! Hope to see you soon," Dicki called while making a double flip in the air.

"Oh yes Dicki, we will see you very soon and thank you for your funny company. Bye bye all you beautiful dolphins."

"It is soooo beautiful to fly above the water," Fleja added as they followed their noses toward the coast of South America, enjoying the timeless space of serenity and unconditional love for all. Halfway there, they met a wonderful school of whales, blissfully radiating healing light through the depths of the water and the atmosphere while rolling and jumping on the surface of the water.

"Hey lovely whales, how are you?" Fleja greeted them.

"Oh hey beloved unicorns! Nice to see you here at the beautiful ocean. We are feeling really blessed and well since the oceans have been purified and are clear again. It is such a joy to live without fear of being hunted or of eating the wrong food such as plastic bottles. We are again able to live our lives as they were always meant to be, simply swimming with joy and fun, radiating love and peace to the world, as well as having lovely friends around us," Pepe, one of the older youngsters, joyfully and wisely answered while racing through the vast ocean below the unicorn family.

"How beautiful to hear that!" Nuja replied as they flew above them, enjoying the peace and love-filled guidance of the beautiful whales.

The sun was still shining as they reached the paradise islands of Hawaii, with its beautiful volcanic soil and mountains and gorgeous sandy beaches.

"Hi happy dolphins!" Fleja called toward some dolphins, who were joyfully diving on the giant waves, playfully sharing them with the surfers around them.

"Hi unicorns, nice to meet you!" Sunny, full of joy, greeted them, still swimming on the crest of the wave.

Shortly afterwards, Fleja and her parents looked for a nice place between beautiful flowers and soft grass to rest for the night, still enjoying the peace and serenity of this paradise island.

10. Andes: A Pair of Condors and Spider Monkeys

After dawn, Fleja, Nuja and Flynn were again in the air, cheerfully continuing their journey toward South America, enjoying the smell of the sea and the stillness of the morning sun. As they reached the landscapes of Chile, a pair of Condors happily joined them and they flew with ease together above the mighty Andes with its beautiful valleys, enjoying the silent and peaceful mountains, where shamanic traditions were being practiced again across the whole continent. The unicorns watched as colorfully dressed shamans gave blessings and natural gifts with love to Mother Earth, thanking her for the nourishment she gives and for their beautiful homes. All families are now living in comfortable, clean houses, enjoying their healthy lives in this wonderful, unique environment. Indeed, magnificent feasts for Mother Earth and the mighty universe were being celebrated everywhere.

"Fleja, Flynn, look. Here is one of the new schools built with natural materials. It has a giant playground and gardens around it – see how beautiful it looks. I am speech-less!" Nuja said.

"Oh, yes, Nuja! That is really fantastic to see. What a joy to see these happy children of all ages playing and learning together in one beautiful, natural place," Flynn answered excitedly, while still spreading his light-filled blessings through his horn over them.

The pair of condors said goodbye as the unicorns followed their instincts to fly toward the vast rainforests. As they saw the first giants of the beautiful jungle trees, they were hearing the joyful and noisy screaming of some of the many species of spider monkeys.

"Hey Mommy, Daddy, what kind of animal is making such a noise?" Fleja asked.

"That must be one of the many groups of monkeys prevalent in the rainforests from Brazil's Atlantic Coast through the southern Amazon to Mexico. You will like them Fleja!" Flynn smiled.

As they reached these wonderful giants of the rainforest, Fleja circled the gorgeous trees, deeply impressed by the majestic and serenity, their power and strength and, of course, the numerous animals living in their branches. "Hey, lovely monkeys! Why are you making such a noise here?" Fleja asked, laughing.

"Hey beautiful unicorn! We are simply having so much fun here jumping and sailing from one branch to the next. It is our unique way of showing our joy, and in the evenings it helps our big family groups reunite for the night's rest."

"Ha ha, that's a really funny way to communicate your happiness." Fleja laughed.

"Yes, of course, we are very funny animals," Tricky, one of the smart spider monkeys, said winking.

Full of love and feeling very lucky, Fleja and her parents journeyed over the vast rainforest.

"Mommy, Daddy, it is amazing here, so colorful and so many different animals live here, wow." Fleja's eyes were open wide.

"Oh, yes Fleja, it really is beautiful here. Since the reforesting program has been established, the animals and nature have been able to recover, and this will continue until it has completely returned to its native state," Nuja said.

"Hmmm, that is great, Mommy, I love it here and I also love the many beautiful and colorful birds … I cannot take my eyes of them," Fleja said, while peacefully following her parents. After a flight with this much joy and ease, the unicorns reached the amazing Machu Picchu by crossing this magical place elegantly with their wondrous wings and sending out rainbow-colored blessings through their horns.

"Nuja, Fleja, let's gather a little more speed and cross Central America with its powerful ancient Pyramids and beautiful countryside and the wonderful cactus deserts of Mexico," Flynn said joyfully, as he started to power up his wings.

11. North America: Eagles, a Herd of Bison, Rabbits and a Pack of Gray Wolves

Enjoying the fresh air again, Flynn, Nuja and Fleja landed in a beautiful meadow below the magical Mount Shasta, watching a wonderful sunset, surrounded by the calmness of this sacred place and enjoying a wonderful sleeping place, too.

"Good morning, Mom and Dad." Fleja woke her parents early the next morning, as she herself was lovingly awoken by the sound of the singing bluebirds flying from one tree to another greeting the new day.

"Good morning Fleja. Thank you, beloved birds, for your wonderful morning song!" Nuja smiled.

After a fresh bath in the lake near the meadow, which was covered with beautiful flowers and encircled by rich green bushes, Fleja and her parents flew slowly toward Yellowstone National Park, meeting Mai and Kirk, a loving pair of eagles, on the way. "Hi, nice to meet you, Mai and Kirk! Come and share this magical journey toward Yellowstone with us," Flynn said.

"It is a pleasure dear Flynn to join you and your family," Kirk answered.

"Ahhh, see, Fleja, Nuja, Mai, Kirk … the first bison are below us. They are one of the vast herds that are again popular from Yellowstone all the way to the north of Canada. What a delight to see them freely wandering in vast herds through the prairie."

"Yes, Flynn. Such a sight brings delight to the heart and soul. We are all so happy that nature is blooming and growing again all over the country. These wonderful bison are able to find food everywhere, just as it has always been."

"Mommy, Mommy, look. There are dozens of rabbits joyfully hopping over the grass," Fleja said happily.

"Yes Fleja, they are enjoying the fresh morning dew on the meadow." Nuja said, watching them with a smile in her face.

After a short flight, the unicorns and pair of eagles reached Yellowstone National Park, a place where all animals can find a calm, nurturing and silent place to recover. Over the past centuries, these animals have been rising up from these magical places all over the countryside. At a wonderful place at the foothills near a forested plateau, Flynn, Nuja and Fleja rested for the day, watching a giant sunset as well as being reintroduced to packs of gray wolves in the early evening hours.

The unicorns said goodbye as the eagles flew an extra cycle over them. After the sun had set and the moon and stars had lit up the sky, a wonderful pack of gray wolves silently appeared in the meadow near the forest, enjoying the peace and serenity of the early night and starting to howl toward the magnificent moon. Fleja, overjoyed, thanked their parents for allowing her to stay awake for so long and be able to watch this awesome, magical spectacle.

The next morning, again lovingly awoken by wonderful singing birds, Fleja, Nuja and Flynn greeted the new day and proceeded on their journey toward the Rocky Mountains and Canada.

12. Canada: A Moose, a Family of Grizzly Bears and a Pair of Falcons

In a beautiful valley in the Rocky Mountains, the unicorn family found a lovely place at a forest's edge beside a giant mountain meadow, blooming with wild flowers of all colors and surrounded by busy bees. With the smell of the different kinds of grasses and flowers in their noses, they elegantly flapped their wings and peacefully landed at the forest's edge.

"Oh, that is beautiful. Come and look. A large moose is watching us through the trees, Daddy." Fleja said.

"Ah, that must be Timo, my wise old moose friend," Flynn said, starting to walk toward the moose.

"Hi Flynn, nice to see you here in my beautiful home," Timo called toward Flynn as he stepped out between the trees.

"Hi Timo, nice to see you, too."

Timo and Flynn greeted each other with great welcoming smiles and a soft touch with the unicorn light from Flynn. "How are you doing, Timo? I see only blooming nature around this awesome countryside! Is all well?"

"Oh yes Flynn, everything is well as you can see. Thanks go to the cleanup of the pollution and, of course, the regrowth of our plentiful food sources through the abandonment of farmland and reforesting management. Here and across the whole landscape, you will see only nature in its unique and original condition. All the wounds that affected the wonderful nature and Mother Earth have vanished forever. Nature has lots of power to recover when it is done in the right way. Nobody was able to imagine this before … it is awesome, Flynn," Timo said.

"Yes, Timo, nature is just amazing."

Simultaneously, Nuja and Fleja, with much joy, examined this comfortable place as Timo and Flynn walked toward them. "Hi Nuja, nice to see you here in my magnificent home," Timo said.

"Hi Timo, nice to see you again. May I introduce you to our daughter, Fleja."

"Hi Fleja, nice to meet you! Hope you will enjoy the nature here."

"Hi Timo, thanks and yes, I like it here, it is so so beautiful."

Just then, in the blooming alpine meadow, Tick and Tack, two funny rabbits, appeared. After a loving and peaceful afternoon together, Timo said goodbye to the unicorn family and walked slowly into the shadows of the forest. Flynn, Nuja and Fleja as well as the rabbits then enjoyed a beautiful sunset and the magic of the falling night. Soon afterwards, they all fell into a deep and healthy sleep.

Early the next morning, shortly after a wonderful sunrise over the alpine meadow, the unicorns proceeded on their journey by following a pure and clean mountain river upstream. As they reached a wonderful and rising waterfall with a giant pond, framed with wild flowers and soft green grass, they joined a magnificent grizzly bear family on the bank, whose children were playing together in the water, watched by their caring mother Ann and father Jim.

"Hi lovely bears," Fleja greeted them, smiling.

"Hi unicorns, nice to meet you," the grizzly family answered.

"Can we join your nice game?" Fleja asked the young grizzly bears in the water.

"Of course, it would be an honor to play with you," said Terry, one of the young grizzly bears.

Fleja immediately joined in and soon was wet from head to toe. "Fleja, would you like to race me in the pond?" Terry asked with a smile.

"With pleasure!"

Terry and Fleja walked to the left edge of the pond. As soon as they started to run, the whole bear family as well as Flynn and Nuja, watching from the bank, was soaked. Shortly before the end of the race circuit, Terry overhauled Fleja and waited happily for his new friend at the finish line.

"Thanks Fleja for the race, it was so funny," Terry said.

"Thanks to you also Terry, I loved it."

Everyone then jumped into the pool, while Flynn and Nuja both offered peace and unconditional love to the bears with their radiant and wondrous horns. Once this funny spectacle had ended, Flynn, Nuja and Fleja took a sunbath in the meadow nearby and once dry, said goodbye to the adoring grizzly bears and flew toward the afternoon sun, crossing the snow-covered and majestic mountains.

They met a wonderful pair of falcons called Rose and Piet, who were waiting for them to join their flight home to the Seventh Heaven. "Hey Flynn, hey Nuja, hey Fleja! Happy to see you again. How was your journey?" Piet asked.

"Hey Piet, hey Rose, so happy to see you again, too. It was just wonderful! Mother Earth and all her wonderful animals have been able to recover and she is blossoming again. It really was a delight to see it with our own eyes as well as to show Fleja a wonderful, peaceful and recovered planet Earth," Flynn said.

"Oh yes Flynn, we are living again on Heaven on Earth. It is awesome how fast everything was able to heal as soon as all humanity learned to respect Mother Earth and all the animals living on her, particularly respecting the soul path of each of them as well as remembering their own soul paths and how to follow them," said Piet wisely with his wide open, all seeing falcon eyes.

Together, Flynn, Nuja, Fleja, Rose and Piet flew home, toward the sun, leaving a magical rainbow-colored path behind them. They quickly vanished with a magnificent light shower behind the sun.

MAY PEACE PREVAIL ON EARTH AND IN OUR HEARTS RIGHT NOW

Andrea Selina grew up at the countryside of South Germany at her grandparent´s small farm. From her beloved grandparents she learned to love every animal as a unique soul and to speak to them like we speak to each others. Also, to take care of them and the commitment to help if needed. After years of working as assistant in the free enterprise she took a break. By searching how to help the beautiful animals on our planet Earth, the story "Heaven on Earth" with Fleja the unicorn child was born.

Zeitfracht Medien GmbH
Ferdinand-Jühlke-Straße 7
99095 Erfurt, Deutschland
produktsicherheit@kolibri360.de